For Evelyn, Lena, Luna, Florez, Sauvira, Aran and their
cousins around the world - *BN*

For Franna, Tobias, Maree and the Munkeys – *PG*

JANETTA OTTER-BARRY BOOKS

Text copyright © Beverley Naidoo 2015
Illustrations copyright © Piet Grobler 2015
First published in Great Britain and in the USA in 2015 by
Frances Lincoln Children's Books,
74-77 White Lion Street, London, N1 9PF

www.franceslincoln.com

A catalogue record for this book is available from the British Library.

ISBN 978-1-84780-514-0

Illustrated with ink, pen, pencil and watercolour

Set in Cochin

Printed in China

9 8 7 6 5 4 3 2

who is King?

TEN MAGICAL STORIES FROM AFRICA

BEVERLEY NAIDOO & PIET GROBLER

Frances Lincoln
Children's Books

Contents

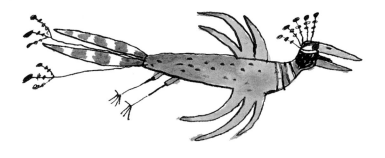

Dear Reader

The word *'Africa'* is short. But can you imagine a bulldozer big enough to dig up China, India, the United States of America and half the countries in Western Europe? Then imagine if we could place all these countries like jigsaw pieces across Africa. They would all fit! The continent in which I was born is HUGE.

Scientists say that Africa was the first home of humans. The human fossils found in the rocks of Ethiopia could be nearly 200,000 years old. When human beings learned to speak, I imagine that they soon started to tell each other stories, weaving them with song and dance. So maybe Africa was the first home of stories.

There are more than 2,000 languages spoken across Africa. Each story here was first told in one of these languages before someone translated it into English. Some of these stories may be thousands of years old. When stories are retold and passed on, bits may get changed. But the heart of a good story lives on.

The animals in these stories are very much like humans. They are at times foolish or wise, mischievous or kind, jealous or generous. They make mistakes and sometimes have to be very brave to get out of trouble. African folktales always invite us to talk about how characters behave.

I hope you will want to hear these tales again... and again. Maybe you will retell them yourselves. You can act them out, with your own singing and dancing. Enjoy them!

Beverley Naidoo

Who is King?

An Amharic tale from ETHIOPIA

Once, Lion wanted to check that all the animals knew who was boss. So he went to each in turn.

"You," he said, starting with Fox. "Who is the king of all the animals?"

Naturally Fox replied, "You, my lord."

Each animal said the same. "You, my lord!"... "You, my lord!"

At last Lion came to Elephant and asked his question.

"Can you come nearer?" Elephant asked.

Lion thought that maybe Elephant was a little deaf. But as he stepped forward to repeat his question, he felt Elephant's trunk grasp him. Next, he was flying high in the sky!

Lion howled as he landed, battered and bruised.

"Why did you do that?" he whined to Elephant. "Why didn't you just say, 'I am the king!'"

Elephant flapped his great ears and raised his trunk. Ignoring Lion, he lumbered away. But he trumpeted loudly to let all the animals know *who* was king.

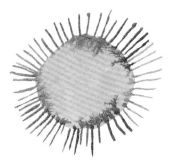

The Ox and the Donkey

An Amharic tale from Ethiopia

Once upon a time an ox and a donkey were friends. Donkey carried the farmer's goods to the market and the farmer didn't overload him. However, Ox found his work of ploughing the earth very tough because the ground was uneven, hard and stony.

One evening, Ox told his friend that he was fed up. "I've had enough of this," Ox complained. "But what can I do?"

"Well, my friend, tomorrow morning let the farmer find you lying on your back and groaning 'Aah! Aah!' as if there's a big pain in your stomach."

So, the next morning, Ox pretended to be sick. "Let my ox rest," said the farmer. "Today I shall use my donkey to plough."

That night Donkey was exhausted, but Ox didn't notice.

"I've had such a lovely day," said Ox. "My good friend, what shall I do to persuade the farmer to let me rest tomorrow?"

"Ah," said Donkey, "haven't you heard? The farmer says he will slaughter you if you can no longer work."

With that, Ox decided it was better to recover!

The Miller's Daughter

An Arabic tale from Morocco

Once upon a time, a poor miller's wife gave birth to a baby girl. The couple named their child Aisha, which means 'she who lives'. Sadly, the baby's mother died and the poor father had no one to help him look after the child while he worked every day.

The miller did his best but he expected that his little daughter might not survive. However, each night when he returned from the mill, he was surprised to find the baby sleeping happily. She had already been fed and washed. Yet no one else was there. Surely, this could only be the work of some good *jinni*!

As the years went by, the child grew into a fine, intelligent girl. Her father could tell that her invisible nurse was also a teacher, because Aisha seemed to know more than a child twice her age. Over the years, the poor miller watched her grow into a beautiful young girl, then a lovely woman. He felt grateful and blessed.

Now the sultan of the land was greatly feared. He would order his soldiers to bring any one of his subjects in front of him, quite randomly. Then the unfortunate person was set an impossible test. The prize was one thousand gold coins, but everyone who failed lost their heads because the sultan proclaimed them 'unintelligent'. So far, every head had rolled.

One day, the soldiers arrived at the mill. Ignoring all protests about the fate of his daughter, they took the poor miller to the palace and pushed him in front of the throne.

"Miller," commanded the sultan, "I have a stream in my garden that turns a mill-wheel. I give you three days to discover what the wheel sings as it turns."

Death pricked the miller's heart. He returned home, sure that he had only three days to live before he would have to say goodbye to his daughter forever.

"Father, why do you look so miserable?" asked Aisha.

When he told her about the sultan's test, Aisha remained calm.

"Don't worry, Father. Just pretend to listen to the mill-wheel and then sing a poem to the sultan. All you need to do is to remember these words." Aisha sang softly and sweetly,

"I was a tree and I was a quince.
My blossoms spread a fine fragrance.
But alas
The sultan took vengeance."

17

Aisha said nothing to her father about the *jinni* whispering in her ear.

On the third day, the miller returned to the sultan. He was escorted to the stream in the palace garden. He crouched down next to the creaking mill-wheel and pretended to listen. Then softly he sang Aisha's poem.

Well, the sultan was taken aback. How did this simple miller know that once there had been a quince tree in the garden? When the sultan had knocked his head against a low branch, he had ordered the entire tree to be hacked down and its wood used for a mill-wheel in his stream.

The sultan didn't allow his subject to see his surprise. Instead, he set a second test.

"Bring me a garden on the back of a camel."

That's impossible, thought the poor miller as he returned home, once again feeling hopeless.

But as soon as Aisha heard the problem, she laughed.

"Father, all you need is a flower box and a camel!"

Before the day was out, the miller led a camel to the palace. On its back, it carried a box filled with soil, blooming with beautiful, bright flowers. This time, the sultan smiled with pleasure. But his smile did not mean that all was well for his poor subject.

"Miller, I have one final test for you. Next time, you must come to me riding and walking, crying and laughing."

The miller sighed deeply as he walked home. Even his clever daughter couldn't possibly solve a riddle like this. Yet when he told it to Aisha, her eyes sparkled.

"At least the sultan has a sense of humour, Father!" As she explained to him what he had to do, even the miller smiled.

The next day at the palace, the sultan waited for the miller. He almost felt a little sorry that he would have to see the miller lose his head. But a test was a test and a rule was a rule. He looked grimly towards the door when his vizier announced the miller's arrival. But why was his vizier's face twisted, as if trying to keep a straight face?

The poor miller was led into the palace garden, sitting on a donkey so small that his feet walked on the ground. The miller himself couldn't help laughing at how silly he felt. At the same time, just as Aisha had advised, his pockets bulged with onions while he peeled another, making tears roll down his cheeks.

At this sorry sight, the sultan burst out laughing. Everyone else now followed suit.

"You are indeed my most intelligent subject!" announced the sultan. "I award you one thousand gold coins."

The miller stepped off the donkey and bowed his head.

"Thank you, your Highness, but Truth makes me confess. Without my daughter's help, I should already have lost my head."

The miller feared the worst as the sultan raised his eyebrows.

"Bring her to me right away," commanded the sultan.

The miller hurried home. What would the sultan do about his deception? He had no choice but to ask Aisha to put on the best of her plain clothes and accompany him to the palace. But when they arrived, they were met by a fanfare and the sultan's vizier led them into a grand banquet room – and a party!

The sultan wished to celebrate his most intelligent subject and spent the whole time talking with Aisha. It wasn't long before he asked her to marry him and legend has it that, under her influence, he changed to become the kindest ruler the people had ever known.

Tortoise and his Banjo

An Igbo tale from Nigeria

Once, in a far, far land, Leopard needed workers for his farm. So he invited all the animals in his town for a work-party. He promised them plenty of food and palm wine if they helped him prepare his land for planting.

Ugbua... Now, I should tell you that Leopard invited everyone except Tortoise. When Tortoise found out, he was very upset. He was also embarrassed that Leopard believed he was too weak for hard work. *Well,* thought Tortoise, *I'll show him!* Without saying a word, he set off to talk with Rabbit in the neighbouring town.

Next morning, all the invited animals gathered at Leopard's farm. Each brought a knife or a hoe. Soon they were busy cutting and digging. They worked hard in the blazing sun. When it was nearly noon, Leopard saw the sweat on their bodies and sent his eldest son home to remind his wives to bring the refreshments.

Ugbua... Now, someone else was digging all that morning. That someone was quietly burrowing an underground tunnel to arrive near Leopard's farm. That someone was Rabbit from

the neighbouring town. He was also working very hard. Tortoise was going to pay him well.

Meanwhile, Tortoise tied his banjo to his back and waited for the dust to settle. When Rabbit announced that he had finished, Tortoise began crawling through his new tunnel. It was noon when he reached the far end. Carefully, he popped his head above the hole. Yes, he was near Leopard's farm – and here was Leopard's eldest son coming along the road! Tortoise slid down out of sight, untied his banjo and began to strum, while singing a little song.

"Poor animals working for Leopard
   Kiri bamba kiri
Silly animals working for Leopard
   Kiri bamba kiri
Drop your hoes, foolish folk
   Kiri bamba kiri
Drop your knives, foolish folk
   Kiri bamba kiri
Save your strength for your own plots
   Kiri bamba kiri
Save your breath for your own crops
   Kiri bamba kiri
Why break your backs for Leopard?"

The music was so mysterious and the melody so enchanting that Leopard's son didn't even listen to the words. His feet began to dance, his body swayed and his head nodded. Whirling and swirling, he completely forgot his father's message.

Very soon, Leopard's son had company. His father's wives hadn't forgotten their task but, as they came from town, they too were charmed by the music. They put down the plates of food and the gourds with palm wine so they could dance more freely. Whirling and swirling.

Ugbua... Now, Leopard was getting anxious. The animals were working more slowly. They kept throwing him glances, expecting him to offer them refreshments. So Leopard kept looking towards the entrance to his farm. Where were his wives? Why hadn't his son returned? Too embarrassed to say anything, he set off to find out.

Well, you can guess what Leopard saw when he began marching down the road. Even from a distance, he recognised the dancers. How dare his wives ignore his orders! In a rage, he stripped a whipping branch from a tree. He would teach them a lesson they wouldn't forget.

However, as the melody wafted towards him, it wove a spell over his feet, body and head. He dropped his whipping branch and began to dance. Whirling and swirling.

Back in the field, the workers were utterly exhausted. Leopard had invited them to a work-PARTY. Where were the refreshments he had promised? How mean of Leopard to lie to them! Stomachs rumbled as the animals grumbled. Finally, taking their knives and hoes, they set off home.

They did not go far before the music wafted towards them. It wove its spell over their feet, body and heads. Their hunger vanished. They too put down their tools and began to dance. Whirling and swirling.

Ugbua... Now, Tortoise peeped out. With everyone there, he plucked the strings faster, adding thrills and trills. He began to sing his song more loudly, more clearly. As the workers danced, they heard the words and each felt a little foolish. *Why break your backs for Leopard?*

Tortoise carried on playing until he sensed that the dancers were weary. Suddenly the music stopped. The spell broke and Tortoise emerged from his hole. He fixed his eyes on Leopard.

"You didn't invite me to work for you, Leopard. So, you see, I had to invite myself."

It was now Leopard who felt foolish. He didn't say anything.

"You told everyone I was weak."

Leopard remained silent.

"Am I and my banjo not strong enough to break your plan?"

Leopard still said nothing.

"Next time, I hope you will not forget the needs of all your fellow creatures."

With that, Tortoise turned to the animals from his town. "Goodbye, Leopard's workers! Goodbye, my dancers!"

Tortoise waved, slung his banjo on his back and descended into his tunnel. It was the shortest way home. The other animals also set off along the road home. It would be a long time before Leopard was allowed to forget his mistake because, every now and again, he would hear someone singing,

"Kiri bamba kiri

Why break your backs for Leopard?"

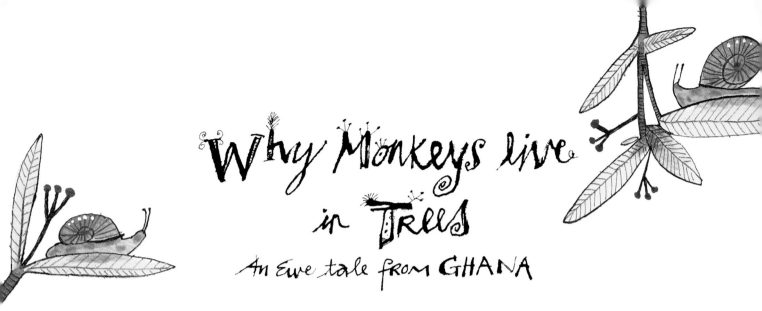

Why Monkeys live in Trees
An Ewe tale from GHANA

Bush Cat was hunting all day. She pounced here, leaped there, but she was unlucky and caught nothing. Even though fleas kept pestering her, she didn't flick them away with her long tail as she didn't want to give away her hiding place. But it was no use. In the end, tired and hungry, she curled up against a cocoa tree with the fleas still feasting on her.

After a little while, Bush Cat saw a monkey sauntering by.

"Monkey, please come and pick out my fleas!" she called.

"Of course, my friend," Monkey said sweetly. "That is what friends are for."

So Monkey sat himself next to Bush Cat and his nimble fingers began trapping and squeezing the fleas. With Monkey combing through her hair, Bush Cat relaxed and began dreaming. She would have better luck tomorrow! Soon, she was fast asleep.

It was night-time when Bush Cat awoke. Monkey was no longer there and the moment she tried to stand up, she knew something was wrong. She could hardly move. Her tail was tied to the tree!

Monkey had played a mean trick! However much Bush Cat pulled, it was no use. In fact, the knot became tighter.

At last, Bush Cat saw a snail crawling a short distance away.

"Snail, please come and untie my tail!" she called.

"How do I know you won't kill me if I untie you?" Snail replied. "You look lean and hungry."

"It's true that I'm very hungry, but I won't harm you," promised Bush Cat.

So Snail bravely untied the knot. Bush Cat thanked her and hurried home.

Next morning, Bush Cat summoned all her friends and told her story. "In five days from now, I want you to announce that I am dead and that you are going to bury me. Make sure that Monkey is invited to my funeral."

Bush Cat's friends agreed and, on the fifth day, they did just as they had been told. Now Bush Cat lay down, very still, pretending to be dead. When her friends began to dance around the body, the other animals followed them, including Monkey.

Suddenly, Bush Cat sprang up, pouncing towards Monkey. But as Bush Cat leaped, Monkey jumped high into a huge silk-cotton tree. It was much too tall for Bush Cat to climb.

So Monkey escaped. But he knew that if Bush Cat ever caught
him on the ground, it would be the end of him.

That's why, since that time, monkeys have lived in trees!

Why Hippo has no hair

A Luo tale from KENYA

A long time ago, Hippo and Fire were friends. They used to meet in the forest. At night, Hippo would trot up from the river, through the long grass and into the forest. Fire burned modestly, but with enough brightness for Hippo to find his way. The friends liked to tell each other stories and they always had something new to share before Hippo would amble back home.

One day, Hippo felt it was time to invite his friend to his own home. He didn't want Fire to think that he was mean.
Well, Fire was very happy. "May I come tomorrow?" he asked.

Hippo replied that would be fine and left the forest a little earlier than usual. He wanted to check that his house was neat and tidy.

Fire's mind was ablaze. This was his first invitation! It took him a while to fall into a deep sleep. By the time he woke up, it was already mid-morning, so Fire hurried to get ready. He didn't want to be late for Hippo.

As he slipped out of the forest, his spirits lifted. Wasn't this exciting? Long grey-green grass, dotted with bushes, stretched all the way down to the river.

However, as soon as he skipped into the grass, a bush in front of him began running away.

"Why are you running away?" called Fire.

"You know why I'm running!" the bush shouted. "Look, the grass is running too!"

Sure enough, the grass was now also running away. Both the bush and the grass were hurrying in the direction of the river.

"Wait for me!" Fire exclaimed. "I'm going to visit my friend Hippo."

"Stop following us!" cried the bush and the grass. "You're too hot! You're hurting the little animals that live with us. You'll kill them. Go away!"

The bush ran as fast as he could but Fire darted faster and ate him. He swallowed all the tiny animals too.

"Please turn back!" screamed the grass, but Fire leaped onwards.

"Hippo is waiting for me. I can't disappoint him," Fire shouted to the grass. He raised his voice above the roaring in his ears. The roaring grew even louder as Fire caught up with the grass. He ate that too and all the bushes that got in his way.

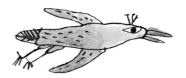

By now, Fire could now see Hippo in the distance, standing next to his house beside the river.

"Don't worry! I'm coming!" he called above the roar.

But Hippo was worried. He could see how Fire was eating everything in his way. What was he to do? Hippo had never seen Fire behave like this. He just hoped that Fire would have eaten enough and calmed down before he reached his home.

When Fire arrived, Hippo smiled nervously.

"Won't you invite me inside?" said Fire.

Hippo was too embarrassed to say "No", so he led the way.

"What a very nice house," said Fire. "I like it."

Now that they were both inside, Fire was very near Hippo who began to feel terribly hot. Yet he didn't want to be rude or show that he was afraid.

"Please sit down," Hippo invited politely.

"Where would you like me to sit?" replied Fire, remembering his manners.

"On my bed," said Hippo.

But Hippo's bed was made of dry grass. As soon as Fire sat down, it burnt underneath him and he ate it all. Fire tried to jump up but then the wall made of reeds caught alight. So did the roof made of thatch. In no time, the whole house was burning.

Poor Hippo knew that he must run away.

But being fat, it was difficult get past
Fire to reach the door. Never before had he
felt so hot and so frightened. From head to tail,
Hippo's hair was now alight, burning orange
and red.

At last, Hippo escaped, just as Fire's flames
began licking his skin.

"Help!" he howled. "My eyes are stinging.
I can't see."

But there was no friend to help him, so he
shambled off as best as he could to the river, and threw
himself in. As he sank down, Water smothered Fire.
Hippo's sighs could be heard far and wide.

From that time on, Water became Hippo's best friend.
Never again did he visit Fire and now you know why hippos
have no hair.

How Elephant got his trunk

a VENDA tale from SOUTH AFRICA

Long, long ago, some animals didn't look like they do today. One of these was Ndou the Elephant. You see, in the beginning, Ndou had a short snout. This made eating very hard work. Elephants couldn't reach the tastiest leaves at the tops of trees. It was also tricky for such big animals to bend down and snuffle out the best shoots under small bushes near the ground.

This wasn't the only problem with short snouts. Elephants need to drink a lot of water. So they had to kneel down beside the waterhole or river to swallow the many mouthfuls they needed. It was even worse in the dry season when everything dried up.

So it happened that one year, after many moons without rain, a herd of elephants trekked over the mountains, hoping to find water in the valley on the other side. They were relieved to glimpse water shimmering in the distance. It was a lake. Their great feet churned up the dust as they hurried towards it.

As the elephants dropped to their knees and sank their snouts into the water, a hungry crocodile slunk silently towards them.

Lifting one eye above the surface, he eyed a young bull elephant who kept himself slightly apart from the others. Crocodile lunged. Razor-sharp teeth sank into snout. So began a fearful tug-of-war.

The young bull, Ndou, was furious. How dare Crocodile sneak up like that! How mean not to share this water! How dare Crocodile make fun of his snout! Every time Crocodile pulled, trying to drag him into the water, Ndou heaved and hauled. With all his might, he tried to get away, trying to ignore the terrible pain.

But something strange was happening. With each tug and yank, Ndou felt his snout stretch. Little by little, it was becoming longer... and longer... and longer! Now it was no longer a snout, it was a nose and, after a while, it was no longer a nose, it was... a trunk!

The sun had been high in the sky when the tug-of-war began. Now the sun was deep red, slipping behind purple hills. Crocodile felt himself lose his grip. There would be no young elephant for dinner. As Crocodile unclenched his jaws, Ndou jolted backwards – suddenly free!

Some other elephants had stayed close to the young bull, trying to support him during the long tug-of-war. They helped him up onto his feet. But when they saw that his snout was now a long, narrow tube, almost reaching the ground, they couldn't help laughing. How funny!

Poor Ndou felt very upset, especially when he looked at his reflection in the water. His nose was tender and sore. It was also very wobbly and, at first, he couldn't control it.

He kept away from the others, who couldn't help staring at the strange long trunk.

But little by little, Ndou began to learn what he could do with his trunk. He was soon collecting the juiciest leaves and berries high up in trees. It was easy to uproot sweet young grasses from the ground and winkle out fresh shoots hidden under dense bushes. When it came to drinking, he no longer had to kneel down like all the others. He could simply slurp up what he needed and squirt the water into his mouth. He could even slosh water over himself to keep cool!

The other elephants soon noticed. Instead of laughing at the young bull, they now began to envy him. Ndou even began to enjoy showing off his trunk-tricks and skills. Then, one by one, at night, elephants began to disappear and return in the morning without a snout but a trunk instead! Each looked very tired, and a bit sheepish, but happy.

Was it always the same old crocodile who offered the tug-of-war? We don't know. If it was, he must have become very, very hungry indeed. Nowadays, elephants are born with trunks, but they still use their mouths to suckle from their mothers and to drink from a waterhole. It takes a little time to learn how to use a long, wobbly trunk.

Unanana and One-Tusk

A Zulu Tale from South Africa

A long time ago, as the rising sun chased away the night's dark cloak every morning, a woman called Unanana left home to work in her field. She only returned as the sun lay down to rest. Even then, she still had to collect firewood from the bush on her way home.

It was very hard for Unanana because her husband was dead. She had two little children to feed, as well as herself and her brother's daughter. This young girl looked after her little ones while she was away. No one in the nearby village offered to help her.

All day, while digging, hoeing and weeding, Unanana hummed the lullaby that she sang every night to her infants.

She imagined their gentle faces and smiles, and this gave her strength.

"Thulani bantwana, ningakhali
Thulani bantwana, lalani
Hush children, don't you cry
Hush children, sleep"

One day, Unanana was in her field, and the children were playing outside their mother's hut, when a large shaggy Baboon, lolloping between some trees, suddenly stopped to stare at them.

"Such beautiful children!" he barked to the young girl in the doorway. "Who is their mother?"

"Unanana! She'll come home soon," the niece said quickly.

"Well, take good care of them," Baboon grunted, before loping on his way.

The following day an Impala, leaping through the bush, stopped to stare. Impala pointed his swirly horns towards the infants.

"Such beautiful children! Who is their mother?"

"Unanana! She'll be home soon," replied the niece.

"Well, take good care of them," Impala yapped, before bounding onwards.

The next day, when a passing Leopard stopped to stare, Unanana's niece was truly nervous.

"Such beautiful children! Who is their mother?" Leopard growled.

"Unanana! She's on her way," the niece said loudly.

"Well, take good care of them," snarled Leopard, before prowling off through the long grass.

Now, Unanana was thankful that these animals admired her children and wouldn't harm them. But no one in the nearby village had warned her that her hut was built on an ancient elephant path. Although most elephants would walk to one side, this was not the case with One-Tusk. Ever since a greedy hunter had stolen one of his ivory tusks, One-Tusk didn't trust any creature on two legs.

So, one day, when One-Tusk came along the path and saw Unanana's hut in the way, he stormed towards it, trumpeting loudly. Unanana's niece had no time to pick up the children.

She ran, screaming, as the angry elephant swept up both infants with his trunk, opened his mouth and swallowed them. In an instant they were gone, and One-Tusk lumbered on his way.

Hearing the rumpus, Unanana dropped her hoe in the field and ran home. It was deserted! A little later, she found her terrified niece shivering and crying in the bush. Her heart turned icy cold when she heard what had happened. Was it possible that her children had been swallowed whole?

Unanana hurried into her hut to fetch her large cooking pot. It contained last night's bean stew. She emerged with the pot on her head, steadying it with one hand, while in the other she carried a long sharp knife. Without a word, she began to follow One-Tusk's tracks.

Before long, she saw Baboon sitting on a rock and called out to him. Had he seen One-Tusk?

"Look for the place of tall trees and white stones," barked Baboon, trying to make his voice soft. He guessed what had happened to the beautiful children.

Some way on, Unanana saw Impala and asked the same question. Impala gave the same answer. His large brown eyes showed sympathy. Yet further on, Unanana saw Leopard stretched along the branch of a tree. Fearlessly, she called out her question.

Leopard flicked his tail to point the direction.

"Find the place of tall trees and white stones," Leopard purred.

Sure enough, in a little while, Unanana saw a clearing of tall trees and large white stones. There, in the middle, stood an enormous elephant with a single tusk. Unanana walked right up in front of him. She waved her knife.

"You swallowed my beautiful children! Give them back to me!" she demanded.

Now One-Tusk didn't like being talked to in this manner, especially by a creature on two legs, like the thief who had stolen his tusk. Was this not also the one who had blocked the elephant path? While One-Tusk began to flap his vast ears, Unanana carried on shouting at him.

Suddenly, he swooped her up with his trunk, shoved her into his mouth and in one gulp sent her flying down, down, down his throat.

Well, this was just what Unanana wanted. Gripping her pot and her knife, she was still in one piece. Now she must find her children! Here was a strange land of valleys and hills dotted with caves full of people, goats, dogs, cats... and there ahead of her were her two children running after some chickens! When she called their names, they turned and came scampering up to her, complaining that they were hungry.

Unanana put down her pot and began feeding her children the bean-stew. In an instant, everyone crowded around her, begging for food.

"Go and build a fire! Can't you see you have meat all around you to roast?" Unanana said scornfully. She recognised some people who had never offered her any help when her husband died.

"Why didn't we think of that?" they said.

In no time, a fire was roaring. The flames rose up higher and higher inside the great beast's stomach. Soon it was One-Tusk who was roaring. He felt a terrible burning inside him and there was nothing he could do to stop it. With a mighty thump, he fell down and died.

It was just in time for all the people inside, who were getting very hot.

Unanana took her knife and swiftly cut a passage between One-Tusk's ribs, leading the way with her children to their world outside. That evening, Unanana received many praises and gifts for freeing everyone.

From then on, the villagers offered her help. Unanana's niece even had a little time to play with the other children. It is also said that elephants have never swallowed people since then. But it is wise for people to show elephants the respect they deserve and, most of all, never to steal their ivory tusks.

Why Cockerel Crows

A CHICHEWA tale from MALAWI

A long time ago, Hyena and Cockerel were friends. Hyena could easily have pounced on Cockerel and eaten a good meal, but the idea never crossed his mind. You see, Hyena felt it was an honour to be Cockerel's friend because, in those days, Cockerel was regarded as highly as Lion and Elephant.

Lion was admired for his strength and Elephant was admired for his size. Yet Cockerel was neither strong nor enormous. Instead, he was respected because of the red comb that flared like spikes of flame on his head. He let everyone believe he could set the world on fire with his comb. So no animal wanted to offend him.

Of course, Cockerel was very happy. He was especially happy when Hyena offered to hoe his field for him without any payment.

Soon, it wasn't only hoeing. Hyena would fetch Cockerel's water and firewood and sweep his yard every day. So Hyena had less time for his own family.

But when his wife questioned him, he was quick to reply,

"Don't you see that it's a great honour for me and our family?"

Now, one day, Hyena came home very late from hunting. Fortunately, he brought a large piece of antelope, left over by Lion. Hyena's family was terribly hungry and his wife wanted to roast the meat immediately. She hurried to the fire she had made earlier that evening but, to her dismay, she found all the embers were dead.

"Look!" she complained to Hyena. "You spent so long helping Cockerel today that our fire has died!"

"Don't worry," said her husband, picking up a stick. "I shall go and ask Cockerel to light this tinder with his comb."

But when Hyena came to Cockerel's home, he found him fast asleep. Surely Cockerel wouldn't mind if he just lightly touched his comb with the dry stick? So he tiptoed up to the sleeping bird, and tried to light the tinder. He tried three times. Nothing happened. There was not a single spark of fire. For the first time, doubt crept into Hyena's mind as he sloped home to face his hungry family.

The next morning, Hyena bowed humbly in front of Cockerel. "What may I do for you today, Sir?"

Cockerel announced a list of jobs.

"It will be my pleasure, Sir. But may I be so bold as to make a request? May I brush your coat today? I would love to make your

feathers truly shine in the sunlight."

Hyena had never offered to do this before. Cockerel was flattered and agreed. Hyena stepped up close to brush the feathers. Instead, pretending to lose his balance, Hyena touched Cockerel's comb. Again, there was no sign of fire.

"Cheat! Imposter!" shouted Hyena, lunging at Cockerel who flung out his wings and flew into a tree, crowing wildly. For the first time, Cockerel revealed his awful singing voice. If he hadn't escaped, Hyena would have torn him to pieces.

Word spread quickly about Cockerel's deception. His hens could no longer bask safely in his glory. The animals were so angry that Cockerel's family had to escape to the village of people. Cockerel was only allowed to stay there after he promised to wake up the villagers by crowing every morning.

And his hens? Well, they had to work for their keep by laying eggs for people to eat. Listen carefully to their clucking and you can sometimes hear them recalling the good old days in the bush.

the Mouse-child

a shona tale from Zimbabwe

Once upon a time, after a long year of drought, there was a woman who had no children. Hunger had stolen her two babies. By the time the rains returned and the new corn grew, it was too late to save her young ones.

One day, the woman saw a little mouse playing near her house. It was chasing its shadow. *I know*, thought the woman, *I shall keep this small mouse and look after it as a pet. It will give me company so I won't feel so lonely.*

Now, every day, when the woman came back from her field, her husband used to scold her.

"Why do you take so long to cook my food? Look at the dust in your house? Aren't you ashamed?"

She remained quiet, feeling sad. She did not remind him that most women in the village had children who helped them with their housework. But, after a while, she had an idea.

"Chikonzo!" she called, for that was the name she gave her pet mouse. "Chikonzo, my little one, would you like to be my own child?"

"*E-ee! Yaa!*" squealed Chikonzo. "That will be fine!"

So, from that day on, the little Mouse called its new mother "*Amai*", which made her very happy. Also, when she returned home every day from working in her field, she was very pleased to see that all her housework was done. The corn was ground into flour. The floor was swept. The food was cooked. Everything was just right!

Now, there were children in the village who were curious about the Mouse-Child. Naturally, they wanted to play with it and, every day, they came and sang in the yard.

"*Come dance with us, Chikonzo, dance!*
To and fro, tsetse ture
No, Amai will scold me if I stop my grinding
To and fro, tsetse ture
Come run with us, Chikonzo, run!
To and fro, tsetse ture
No, Amai will scold me if I stop my sweeping
To and fro, tsetse ture
Come play with us, Chikonzo, play!
To and fro, tsetse ture
No, Amai will scold me if I stop my cooking
To and fro, tsetse ture."

So the song went on, but all the while little Chikonzo was busy grinding, sweeping, cooking and taking care of the house until the work was finished. Afterwards, Chikonzo joined the children in games of chasing and hiding.

One day, when Chikonzo's mother came home, she found all the children in her yard. Inside her house, everything was fine, but suddenly other women of the village arrived. They were the children's mothers.

"Where have you children been all day?" they shouted. "You never ground the corn! You didn't make the fire! You never cooked! You never swept! What are you doing here?"

The children were too frightened to say anything about their new friend and hurried home to do their work. But they came back the next day and, even though they watched Chikonzo working, they enjoyed themselves singing and forgot the time.

When their mothers found the housework not done again, they were furious. This time, they caught the children and threatened to beat them. Now the children confessed.

"We came to watch Chikonzo, the Mouse-Child that grinds the corn, cooks the food and sweeps the floor!"

But that made the mothers more furious. As they dragged their children away, they shouted, "Why do you lie to us? Do you think we are stupid to believe such nonsense?"

So it went on until, one morning, an elder of the village decided to find out what was really happening. The old man waited until he saw the woman set off with her hoe for her field. Quietly, he strolled closer so he could see inside her house. *Yaa!* There was the mouse grinding corn! He watched it sweep the floor before he called the husband.

"Come and see who is doing your wife's work!"

When the husband arrived and saw the busy mouse, he was very angry.

"Yo! I see with my own eyes! My wife is so lazy that she has this creature to do her housework. I'll teach her a lesson!"

The next day, after his wife left for the field, he slipped into her house, grabbed the mouse and took it to the bush, saying,

"Don't come back."

When the woman returned home, everything was just as she had left it in the morning. The grindstone wasn't touched... the fire wasn't made... the pot was empty... the floor wasn't swept... and *where* was her Chikonzo? As she made the fire, her eyes filled with smoke. Her tears fell.

Her husband found her there, and asked,

"Why are you crying?"

"I'm not crying. It's just the smoke in my eyes," she replied.

Suddenly, her husband felt bad.

He remembered the two small children taken by Hunger.

"I know," he said, "you are crying because you have lost your child. I took away your mouse and it was your child. Now I understand. I shall go and bring your Mouse-Child back."

So her husband went into the bush. He found the mouse exactly where he had left it, with its head bent down. It hadn't moved. He carried it carefully back to his wife and, as soon as Chikonzo saw her stirring the pot, it leapt out of the husband's hand and hurried to bring more sticks for the fire.

From that time on, the Mouse-Child did all the housework. It ground the corn, cooked the food, swept the floor and it taught the children how to do their own housework so there was also time for play.

Now everyone was happy... and that is where this story ends.

About the Stories

I thank all the storytellers and translators who have kept these stories alive for centuries, as well as giving special thanks to the storytellers and collectors below:

'The Ox and the Donkey' comes from the storyteller Melese Getahun Wolde and 'Who is King?' comes from Chilot Amara, who calls his story 'The King of the Animals'. These two Ethiopian folktales were collected by Elizabeth Laird and translators for a unique storytelling project from 1997 to 2001. You can read about it, as well as many more stories at www.ethiopianfolktales.com.

The Moroccan story of 'The Miller's Daughter' appears in *Kings, Gods & Spirits from African Mythology* by Jan Knappert (Eurobook, 1986). It is fascinating to compare this with 'Rumpelstiltskin' by the Brothers Grimm, a European fairytale about a miller who boasts that his daughter can spin gold.

The tale from Ghana, 'Why Monkeys Live in Trees', appears in *African Folktales*, a collection of nearly a hundred stories retold by the well-known American folklorist Roger D Abrahams (Pantheon Books, 1983). This is also where I found 'Tiger slights the Tortoise', from Nigeria. But as there are no tigers in Africa, I changed Tiger into Leopard in my retelling, 'Tortoise and his Banjo'.

Pamela Kola tells her grandmother's story of 'Why the hippo has no hair' in *East African Why Stories* (East African Educational Publishers, 1991). When she was growing up near Lake Victoria, Pamela listened to her grandmother

telling stories in their language, Luo, especially at night around the fire. As an adult, she began translating and writing these tales in English so that children and adults across east Africa and beyond could enjoy them. Pamela Kola is a founder member of Kenya's National Book Development Council.

'Why Cockerel Crows' comes from *An Anthology of Malawian Literature for Junior Secondary* (Dzuka Publishing Co, 1993). The editors Christopher F. Kamlongera and Wales B. Mwanza call it 'Cockerel becomes a domestic bird' which is another theme in the story.

In 'The Mouse-Child', I retell the Zimbabwean story 'The Woman and the Mouse' from *The Lion on the Path and other African stories* by Hugh Tracey (Routledge and Kegan Paul, 1967). When I was young, my parents took me to meet Hugh Tracey at his farm in South Africa. He collected and made traditional musical instruments, and was well-known for recording African folk music so it could be heard by future generations. Most of the stories he collected and told had songs in them.

Nick Greaves includes the South African stories 'Why Elephant has a Trunk' and 'Unanana and the Wicked One-tusked Elephant' in *When Elephant was King* (Struik Publishers, 2000). Although I changed the titles slightly, I hope the spirit of each story lives on.

I also thank Maren Bodenstein and Mary Stuart for help with isiZulu.